The Adventure · of the · BIG SNOW

Nancy McArthur

illustrated by Mike Reed

A
LITTLE APPLE
PAPERBACK

New York   Toronto   London   Auckland   Sydney

To Daniel McArthur and Timothy McArthur

ISBN 0-590-37209-2

Text copyright © 1998 by Nancy McArthur.
Illustrations copyright © 1998 by Scholastic Inc.
All rights reserved. Published by Scholastic Inc. LITTLE APPLE PAPERBACKS and logos are trademarks of Scholastic Inc.

12 11 10 9 8 7 6 5 4 3 2 1   8 9/9 0 1/0

Printed in the U.S.A.   40

First Scholastic printing, February 1998

1

Susie looked up from her worksheet. Tiny white flakes whirling outside the classroom window had caught her eye.

She whispered to Megan, "It's snowing."

Megan looked. She grinned and nodded.

Susie said loudly, "It's snowing!" Everyone turned to look out the window.

Eric said, "I don't see any snow."

Their teacher, Mrs. Hansen, said, "There *are* snowflakes — just a few."

Tim said, "Maybe it'll snow so much we won't have school tomorrow." Everybody laughed. Susie wished that would happen. Then she wouldn't have to give her book report tomorrow. Book reports made her nervous.

Mrs. Hansen smiled. "We hardly ever get much snow this early in winter," she said.

Soon it was time to go home. The bus riders lined up and marched out. The walkers got ready to go.

"See you tomorrow," said Mrs. Hansen.

In the hall, Susie's and Megan's friend Annie waited for them. They all lived on the same street. They walked home together every day.

Now big fluffy snowflakes filled the air. Icy wind sneaked down Susie's coat collar. She yanked her knitted hat down over her ears.

"It's really cold," said Annie.

"I hope it snows a lot," said Megan. "Then we can build a fort and a snowman."

"I hope it snows a *really* lot," said Susie. "Then we won't have school tomorrow."

Eric and Tim ran past them. "If it keeps snowing," Eric called to Tim, "let's build a fort."

Tim shouted, "And a snowman!"

"Rats!" said Susie. "They thought of it, too."

Annie said, "We thought of it first."

The edges of the grass by the sidewalk were getting white. The girls ran most of the way home.

Susie's fuzzy brown dog, Puddles, heard the back door open. He knew whose footsteps those were. His favorite human was home! He galloped through the kitchen. Pud was so glad to see Susie that he wiggled all over. She dropped her backpack and hugged him.

Next door at Megan's, her big orange cat, Fluffo, rubbed against her leg. She scratched under his chin. Fluffo loved that. It felt so good.

The back door banged open. Freezing air blew in with Megan's teenaged brother, Mike.

He dropped his coat and backpack on the

floor. He got out a bunch of snacks and took them to the table.

"I hope we get a blizzard," he said. "Dad said I can run the snowblower this year. I can make lots of money clearing walks and driveways."

"Susie and Annie and I are going to build a fort and a snowman," said Megan.

Mike smeared peanut butter on three crackers. He stuffed them all into his mouth at once.

"I used to do those things when I was a kid," he mumbled with his mouth full.

Megan sat down and reached for the snacks. Fluffo jumped up on the chair between them.

"Hey, Mr. Fluffaduff," said Mike. "Here you go." He handed him a little piece of chicken.

The three of them sat sharing their snacks and watching the snow fall.

Megan crumpled a paper wrapper from the cracker box. She tossed it to Fluffo. The cat knocked it to the floor. He jumped down and pounced on it. He knocked it across the room.

He leaped after it. He batted it into the air and chased after it. Mike and Megan chuckled at his antics.

"Mr. Fluffaduff," said Mike, "you're better than cartoons."

2

Susie pressed her cold feet against the kitchen heating vent. Warm air blew up from the furnace in the basement.

Pud wanted his afternoon walk. He trotted to the door. He trotted to Susie. He nudged her knees and ran back to the door. Why wasn't she getting his leash? She just stood there, toasting her toes.

Susie's mom reminded her, "It's your job to take Pud out after school."

"It's too cold," whined Susie. "I don't want to get my toes froze."

Mom replied, "You don't have to go far. Just take him around the yard."

Susie bundled up. She put on her new winter boots, her coat, hat, scarf, and mittens.

Out into the cold went Susie and Pud. Now the grass was all white.

The dog eagerly hurried across the yard. He pulled Susie along with the leash.

Pud stopped to sniff the ground. Dogs can detect smells that humans don't know are there. His nose told him that squirrels had been here not long ago. Pud liked to chase squirrels. He didn't want to catch them. He liked to make them run up trees.

Pud's nose also told him that the nosy orange cat from next door had been here again. Pud wanted that cat to stay out of his yard.

He caught a whiff of a different cat. He tugged on the leash to follow that smell. It led toward the garage. But Susie pulled him away into their other next-door neighbor's backyard.

Mrs. Johnson was scooping seeds into her

bird feeder. It hung on a rope from a tree branch. Snowflakes were sticking to her hat and coat.

"Hi, Susie," she said. "It looks like we might get a big snow, doesn't it?"

Susie replied, "I hope we get a snow day off from school."

Mrs. Johnson said, "If you do, come over. I might have some jobs if you want to earn a little money."

Susie led Pud back to their own yard. He tried again to follow the smell of the strange cat.

Susie thought he wanted to growl at the thick evergreen bushes by the garage. Fluffo must be lurking under there again. It was one of the cat's favorite hiding places.

"No," Susie told Pud. She pulled the leash the other way. So they did not go near the bushes. They did not see the little gray kitten huddled there in the cold.

* * *

Susie's dad was late getting home. He came in, stamping snow off his shoes.

"The roads are slippery," he said. "The radio said it's going to snow all night."

Susie kept running to the TV to see if there was any news about no school tomorrow.

After dinner, it was time for Pud's evening walk. This was Dad's job. Susie went along.

The wind had died down. It was very quiet outside. The softly falling snow was getting deeper. Susie's feet sunk in up to her ankles. The only marks in the snow were their footprints — Dad's big boots, Susie's small ones, and Pud's paws. Their warm breath made little clouds in the frosty air.

Lighted windows of the houses they passed shone on the white front yards.

Dad scooped up a handful of snow. He pressed it into a ball.

"This is good packing snow," he said. "Not too wet. Not too heavy. Just right." He threw the snowball ahead of them. Pud dashed after it. When he got to it, it had fallen apart. Pud couldn't figure out where the white ball had gone.

At Megan's, Fluffo waited by the back door to be let out. He liked to go prowling at night.

Megan opened the door. "Hurry back," she said.

Fluffo stepped out into snow up to his stomach. He shook one paw, then another. He charged across the yard like a little snow-plow. The ivy in the corner where he always looked for bugs or mice was covered in white.

He stopped to listen. Nothing stirred. Snow fell gently on his fur. He plowed on. He headed straight for the evergreen bushes by the dog's garage.

3

Fluffo crawled under the bushes and got a big surprise.

The kitten went, *"Sissssss!"* right in his face. Fluffo hissed back. They stared at each other. Even when there is hardly any light, cats can see.

Fluffo hissed again. But the kitten did not run away.

At home Fluffo didn't have to put up with hissing kittens. He decided to go back there.

The kitten peeked out to watch where he

went. At the back door Fluffo called loudly, "MEOW! MEOW!"

The door opened. The big cat went inside. The kitten followed. It was hard going through the snow on his short little legs. He made it to the back door.

"Mew!" he cried in his squeaky little voice. "Mew! Mew! Mew!"

Megan opened the door.

"It's a kitten!" she exclaimed. She carried him into the warm kitchen.

Her mother inspected the kitten carefully. "No fleas," she said. "He can't be more than eight or ten weeks old. That's when cats are old enough to leave their mothers to be adopted. It's too bad he doesn't have an identification collar."

"Let's keep him," said Megan.

"No," said her mother. "One cat is enough for us. We'll find a good home for him. We'll ask everyone we know if they want a kitten."

Megan wrapped the newcomer in a towel. She wiped the melted snow from his fur. She scratched under his chin. He purred and licked her hand. She gave him some food.

Fluffo sat under the kitchen table licking the melted snow off his fur. He watched Megan cuddling the other cat. No one was paying any attention to Fluffo.

When Susie, her dad, and Pud were almost home, the streetlights and all the houses went dark.

"Oh, no," said Dad. "The power's gone off!"

Mom met them at the door with a flashlight.

"I hope the electricity won't be off long," she said. "In this weather, we don't want to do without heat."

"No heat?" said Susie. She wanted to toast her toes again by the kitchen vent.

"No," said Dad, "the gas furnace won't work without electricity."

"Neither will our electric stove or the refrigerator," added Mom. "But the phone's still working."

"No TV," added Dad.

Susie asked, "How can I find out if there's no school tomorrow?"

"My radio runs on batteries," said Dad. "We'll listen to that."

Mom lit candles. Dad built a fire in the fireplace. He used twists of paper and twigs to start it. He added logs on top.

Soon the logs began burning brightly.

"This is like olden times," said Susie. "Like

we learned about in school. No electricity. Candles and fireplaces. And no TV."

Mom said, "People used to cook in their fireplaces. And carry water in from outside. They didn't have faucets in the house. I'm glad we don't have to do that."

Dad said, "I read somewhere that in freezing weather people brought their farm animals into their houses."

Mom said, "I'm glad we don't have to do that, either."

Susie pictured what that would look like. Chickens would be sitting on the bookshelves. Or cows on the couch. She giggled.

"We've got Pud," she said. She hugged him.

The phone rang.

"There weren't any phones in olden times," said Dad. He answered it.

"It's for you," he told Susie. "It's Megan."

Megan told her excitedly, "Do you want a kitten? We found one. And we just heard on the radio there's no school tomorrow!"

4

Susie hurried back to the fireplace. The house was getting chilly.

"No school! No school!" she sang.

Dad tuned the radio to a weather report.

The radio said, "As much as three feet of snow is expected by morning. Schools will be closed. Police ask everyone to stay off the roads tonight. Some homes will be without power until tomorrow."

Dad, Mom, Susie, and Pud snuggled together in a row on the couch. Susie tucked her feet under Pud's warm furry belly.

They watched the orange and yellow flames in the fireplace. The burning logs crackled.

Susie said, "Megan asked if we want a kitten. They found one."

"No," replied Mom.

Dad added, "One pet is enough for us."

Pud yawned. He looked like he was nodding his head.

Susie laughed. "He said yes," she said.

After a while, Susie put her head down on Mom's lap. The voices above her sounded farther and farther away. Soon she was asleep.

She woke when Dad carried her upstairs.

"We're all going to sleep with our clothes on," he said. "That'll be warmer." He tucked Susie into her bed. The sheets felt cold.

Pud lay on the rug beside the bed. Dad left a turned-on flashlight in the hall for a night-light.

Susie threw back the covers and patted the mattress. Pud jumped on the bed. She pulled the covers over both of them.

*   *   *

At Megan's, her mother put a towel in a cardboard box for the kitten to sleep in. She left him alone in the dark kitchen.

Upstairs, Fluffo was asleep as usual on Megan's bed. Megan and Fluffo did not stir when silent tiny feet crept into the room. They did not hear tiny claws climbing up the bedspread.

The kitten walked softly across the bed. He lay down near Fluffo. The big cat did not wake up and hiss. The kitten moved closer and snuggled up.

Fluffo sighed but did not wake. Maybe he was dreaming about long ago when he was a kitten. He had nestled with his mother and brothers and sisters in a cardboard box with a towel in it.

5

In the morning, Susie slid out of bed. Her room was very cold. She was glad she didn't have to get dressed. That would give her even more shivers. She hurried to her window. What she saw was beautiful.

Everything was covered deeply in smooth white. The snow sparkled in the sunlight. The street and sidewalks had disappeared under it. The dark trunks of the leafless trees had long blue shadows. Evergreen trees and bushes were bent low by heavy snow on their branches. Roofs looked like the white cake frosting on

gingerbread houses. Wisps of smoke rose from chimneys.

A big yellow snowplow truck came barreling down the street. The huge metal scraper on its front pushed the snow aside. It made giant heaps along where the curbs used to be.

A loud grinding motor started up next door. Susie put her hands over her ears. She saw a plume of snow flying high from where Megan's driveway was buried. A snowblower came into view. Mike was pushing it.

Megan was out playing in her front yard. She sank in up to her hips. Lying on the snow, she flapped her arms. She moved her legs out to the sides and back.

Her legs made a wide dent like a long skirt. Her arms made the shapes of big wings. A snow angel! Susie and Megan and Annie made those every winter.

Susie pulled a blanket off her bed. She wrapped herself in it. It was so cold in the house! She ran downstairs. Her dad and mom were wearing coats. Pud was stretched out in front of the fireplace.

"Let's cook something over the fire," said Dad. "I don't want cold cereal for breakfast. I'm cold enough already."

Susie suggested, "We could toast marshmallows."

"For breakfast?" said Mom. "Yuck."

Dad brought hot dogs and sliced bread from the kitchen.

"Hot dogs for breakfast?" exclaimed Susie. "Yuck!"

Dad said, "Hot dogs roasted over a fire are pretty good eating."

He stuck one on the long two-pronged fork he used for summer cookouts. He held it over the flames. At last the hot dog began to sizzle.

"Now we're cooking!" said Dad. The hot dog smelled good. Pud watched. While they waited, Mom got orange juice for them all.

She said, "We have to have *something* healthy!"

When the hot dog was ready, Dad took it off the fork. He put it aside on a plate.

He put a slice of bread on the fork to toast to go with the hot dog. When it was quickly browned, he turned to get the cooked hot dog. It was gone.

Pud was chewing. Susie laughed.

"He wanted a hot breakfast, too!" she said.

"Bad dog," scolded Dad. He started over with another hot dog. It took a long time to cook breakfast this way. Susie ate her hot dog and three pieces of toast. Mom opened a can of baked beans to go with the hot dogs.

Susie asked, "Now can we have marshmallows for dessert?"

Mom laughed. "We might as well," she said. "This breakfast is already so weird, I guess it won't matter."

Susie held the fork to toast the marshmallows. She held the first one too close to the flames. It caught fire and burned up. The next one she held farther away. It got golden brown and gooey.

"This one's just right," she said. With a lightning-fast chomp, Pud snatched it from her fingers.

"Bad dog!" said Susie. White goo oozed out of one side of his mouth. He licked it up.

Susie started over with another marshmallow.

She said, "This is the silliest breakfast I ever ate."

"Me, too," agreed Mom.

"But at least we had hot food," added Dad.

Pud yawned and nodded. Then he burped.

When Susie went in the kitchen, suddenly the refrigerator started to hum.

"The power's on!" she yelled. She sat down by the heat vent to get warm.

6

When Susie went outside, Mike was snow-blowing at another yard down the street. Megan had gone inside. She had covered her front yard with Megan-sized snow angels. The snowblower had thrown big piles of snow along both sides of the drive and walks.

Susie waded through the snow of her own front yard. She flopped down and made an angel.

She looked around at tiny bird tracks on the snow. Their footprints did not lead anywhere. They had touched down and then flown away.

Susie climbed the heap of snow beside Megan's drive. She slid down the other side. Footprints led to Megan's door. One set was in a straight line from Annie's house across the street.

"Aha!" said Susie. She rang the bell. Megan opened the door.

Susie said, "Annie's here!"

"How did you know?" asked Megan.

"A trail in the snow," replied Susie.

Annie was in the kitchen playing with the kitten. She pulled a piece of string along the floor. The kitten chased and pounced on it. Fluffo watched from under the table.

"Oooh," squealed Susie. "He's so cute!" She squatted down to pat the kitten. She asked Annie, "Are you going to adopt him?"

"I can't," replied Annie. "Cats make my sister sneeze. She's allergic."

Megan said, "Tim's dad and mom said if he likes the kitten, he can have it. He and Eric are coming over — as soon as they finish making their fort. He said they already made their snowman."

She tossed a crumpled paper to the kitten. He pounced. He batted it away and scampered after it. *Whack!* He sent it flying.

It landed under the table beside Fluffo.

Fluffo did not bat it back. He moved over and lay down on top of it.

The kitten looked around. He could not find his toy. He gave up. He went to drink from Fluffo's water dish.

Megan said to Fluffo, "Don't you want to play?"

Fluffo just looked at her.

Susie said, "Let's go build our snowman."

"And our fort," added Megan.

Annie said, "We better hurry up before Eric and Tim get here."

Annie and Susie jumped off the steps into the deep snow in Megan's yard.

Megan yelled, "Don't mess up my snow angels! Oh, no! You already messed them up!"

Susie said, "You've got lots of them! We only messed up a couple. You didn't leave any room to make anything else!" She led the way to her own yard.

They used the high heap of snow along the driveway for their fort wall. They patted it to pack it smooth. Annie made a little border of snow by her feet.

"This is my room divider," she explained. "This is my room." Megan and Susie made their own dividers.

They sat with their backs against the wall. They looked up at the blue sky.

"This is a fort house," said Megan. "We can visit each other's rooms."

Susie and Megan stepped over the dividers into Annie's room and sat down. "This is nice," said Megan.

After a while Susie said, "Let's build our snowman."

They got a shovel and took turns piling and packing snow straight up. Soon the pile was three feet high. For a head, they made a big round ball.

Megan poked dents for two eyes and a nose. She made a curved line for a smiling mouth.

"It's done," she said.

"It's not very big," said Annie.

"It's big enough," replied Susie.

7

Eric and Tim came walking up the middle of the street. The girls let them into their fort.

"Cool," said Eric.

Megan asked, "Does yours have rooms?"

"No," replied Tim. The boys walked around the snowman.

"We built a bigger one in my yard," bragged Eric.

Susie replied, "We *wanted* ours to be shorter."

"Yeah," said Megan. "Ours is shorter 'cause it's not a snow*man*. It's a snow*girl*!"

Susie was glad Megan thought of this.

Tim said, "It still looks like a little snow-*man*."

"She isn't dressed up yet," explained Susie.

"What's she going to wear?" asked Eric.

"A purse," said Susie.

Annie suggested, "She should have long hair. That would look nice. And earrings."

Eric said, "Snowpeople don't have hair. They wear hats sometimes. Ours has a baseball cap and a hockey stick."

Susie pulled off her knit hat. She stretched it to put it on the snowgirl's big head. But when she let go, it popped off. The boys laughed.

"I'm getting a purse," she said. She went in the house.

Susie's mom found an old purse with a long strap for her. Susie saw a bunch of green yarn in a box on the closet floor.

"Can I have that?" she asked.

"Okay," said Mom. "It's left over."

Susie said, "We need some earrings."

"I'm not letting you have any of mine," replied Mom. "How about these old purple earmuffs?"

When Susie got back outside, Megan had tied her own red scarf around the snowgirl's neck.

"That looks good," said Megan.

Tim said, "How's the snowgirl going to hold her purse? She doesn't have any arms." Susie slung the strap around the back of the snowgirl's neck. The purse hung down in front.

"That's how," she said.

Eric asked, "What's the yarn for? Are you going to knit her a sweater?"

"It's going to be her hair," said Susie.

"Green hair?" said Eric, laughing. "Nobody has green hair."

Megan said, "It can be mermaid hair. Like seaweed! She's a snow-mermaid."

"Yes!" said Susie. "A snermaid!" The girls giggled. The boys joined in. Annie helped Susie spread the loops of yarn over the head.

Susie clamped the earmuffs over it.

Annie said, "Mermaids don't wear earmuffs."

"She needs them," explained Susie, "to hold her hair on. So a big wave won't knock it off."

Megan suggested, "The earmuffs can be like her ears."

"Cool," said Annie.

Eric said, "Purple ears! Mermaids don't have purple ears!"

Megan replied, "She's a snermaid. You don't know anything about snermaids. They can have all colors of ears. Even purple."

Annie said, "I think purple ears look nice with green hair."

"Me, too," said Susie.

"Me, too," said Megan.

"It's weird," said Tim.

Megan took her red scarf off the snermaid. "Red doesn't look too good with purple," she said. "Besides, my neck's getting cold."

Tim said, "I want to see the kitten."

8

The kitten and Tim liked each other right away. "I'll take him," said Tim. He tucked the little cat inside his coat to keep him warm on the walk home. He didn't zip the coat all the way up. The tiny gray face poked out and looked around.

Susie thought the kitten looked like a small kangaroo peeking out of a pouch. But she didn't say so.

"You should call him Hoppy," she told Tim.

Megan said, "You should call him Fuzzball."

Annie said, "You should call him Squeaky."

Eric said, "You should call him Batcat."

"Batster Catster!" exclaimed Tim. "I like that. We have to go now," he added. "We're going to shovel snow and earn money."

Megan's mother gave the boys two cans of cat food and a half a bag of cat litter to take along.

"I'm so glad I got this cat," said Tim. "I always wanted one."

Megan's mother said, "We're glad you're giving him a good home."

The girls went outside. They made more rooms in their fort.

Megan said, "We could make money shoveling, too."

Susie said, "We only have one shovel."

"We can take turns," said Annie.

Susie suggested, "Let's go over to Mrs. Johnson's. I do jobs for her."

Megan said, "Mike's going to snowblow for her after lunch."

"We could beat him to it," said Susie.

Annie said, "He can do the driveway. We can do the sidewalk before he gets there."

The girls clomped up the steps to Mrs. Johnson's porch. Susie rang the bell.

"Hey!" yelled a familiar voice behind them. "We're going to shovel there!"

Eric and Tim were coming up the street. They were dragging snow shovels.

"We got here first!" yelled Megan.

The boys hurried up onto the porch.

Tim said, "Mrs. Johnson said we could shovel for her."

"No," said Susie. "You didn't even talk to her yet."

Eric said, "We called her up."

Mrs. Johnson opened the door. "Hello, everybody," she said.

"We want to shovel your sidewalk," said Susie. "We got here first."

"You said we could do it," said Eric.

"Yes," said Mrs. Johnson. "But there's enough snow to go around for everybody. I'll hire you all for the job."

Eric boasted, "We have two shovels. They only have one. So we can shovel twice as much snow. You can pay us twice as much."

Mrs. Johnson decided, "Everyone gets paid the same. Eric, Tim, and Susie, you shovel. Megan, take my broom and push the snow off the porch and steps. A shovel would scrape the paint. Annie, you knock the heavy snow off the evergreen bushes so the branches don't break."

The boys started shoveling the front walk

from the porch steps toward the street. Susie began at the other end of the walk.

Megan swept snow from the top step. It landed where Tim was shoveling next to the bottom step.

"Hey!" yelled Tim. He tossed a shovelful of snow up on the steps.

"Hey!" yelled Megan. She swept more snow right on him. He tossed another shovelful at her. They ducked and threw more snow, shrieking and laughing.

The front door opened. Mrs. Johnson called, "Settle down. I'm not paying you to shovel snow all over each other." They got to work.

9

When they finished, Mrs. Johnson invited them in for cocoa and cookies. She paid everyone. The boys left to find other shoveling jobs. The girls stayed awhile.

Outside Mrs. Johnson's kitchen window, birds fluttered down to her feeder but did not stay. They flew away.

Susie said, "Your feeder's empty."

Mrs. Johnson asked, "Would you fill it for me when you go out?"

* * *

Fluffo was out prowling in Susie's yard. He sneaked up behind the snermaid. He saw the green hair dangling. It fluttered a little in the wind. Fluffo could not resist. He leaped at it. His claws caught the yarn and dragged it down. The earmuffs popped off.

Loops of yarn fell around Fluffo's neck. He bit at the yarn to get his claws unstuck. That didn't work. He tried walking away from the yarn. It went with him.

Fluffo rolled over to try to free himself. His back claws got tangled up, too. He wrestled with the yarn. It got more snarled around him.

He rolled and squirmed and wiggled across smooth snow to his own backyard.

Susie held the big bag of birdseed. Megan held the feeder steady. Annie scooped in the seed.

Susie looked at the bird tracks around them on the snow. There were other tracks, too — paw prints and places where it looked like creatures had sat down. She knew they were not cat or dog tracks.

"These might be rabbit tracks," she said. "Or something else. But they don't come across the yard like ours. See? The mystery tracks are just right here. No place else! It looks like they came from the sky! Like the birds!"

"Flying rabbits?" exclaimed Annie. "That can't be."

Megan said, "Maybe it was a funny kind of bird. One with paws."

Susie said, "Maybe a pterodactyl." She chuckled. "A really little one."

Back in Susie's yard, the girls saw the snermaid.

Susie yelled, "Somebody swiped her hair!" She put the earmuffs back on the head.

Annie said, "Purple ears don't look so good without green hair."

Megan said, "Maybe Tim and Eric took it to play a trick!"

"It must have been them," agreed Annie.

Megan said, "Let's go over to Eric's and see if their snowman has green hair. I bet they wanted to copy us."

Susie looked for footprints. The snow around the snermaid was all trampled down. But nearby, on smooth snow, she saw strange tracks.

"Look!" she said. "Something else was here! Not Tim and Eric!"

"Some THING?" said Annie. Her eyes opened wide. Susie pointed to the odd-looking marks. Paw prints were mixed in with them.

Megan said, "These paw prints could be Fluffo's. Maybe he chased after what took our snermaid's hair." She picked up a tiny piece of bitten-off green yarn.

"The hair went this way!" she called. Annie and Susie followed.

Susie said, "If it was an animal, these big marks must be its feet. Big hairy feet!"

"Maybe it got Fluffo," said Annie, looking worried. "It looks like they were fighting!"

The trail led to Megan's back door. There sat Fluffo — all tangled up in green yarn.

"He's okay!" said Megan.

"He saved the snermaid's hair from the hair stealer monster!" said Susie. "Whatever it was."

Fluffo did not look happy.

Annie giggled. "He's having a bad green hair day," she said.

The girls took Fluffo inside to untangle him.

At Mrs. Johnson's feeder, birds were busy eating. High above in the tree, the mysterious track maker appeared. She had been hiding in her nest.

She was not a little pterodactyl. She was not a flying rabbit. She was a plump squirrel.

She ran headfirst down the tree trunk. She dashed out on the branch where the feeder hung by a rope. The birds flew off.

The squirrel made a flying leap. She clutched the feeder with her front claws. It swung out and back. She gobbled seeds, sailing back and forth like a circus act on a trapeze. With every swing, seeds spilled out.

The squirrel jumped down off the feeder. Eating on the snow was easier than munching while swooping through the air.

Pud came out his back door. Susie's mom was right behind him. But she had not clipped his leash on yet. He saw the squirrel and took off.

The deep snow stopped him from running fast. He kept sinking in up to his stomach.

The squirrel leaped to the tree trunk. She raced up and away. From a high branch she jumped to another tree.

Pud barked twice to show who was boss. But the squirrel hadn't stayed to listen.

Susie went home for lunch. When she came back outside, she saw a small sign on a utility pole. It hadn't been there before. The hand-lettering said:

There was a phone number at the bottom.

"Uh-oh," said Susie.

She hurried to Megan's with the news.

10

"Oh, dear," said Megan's mother. "I thought finding a home for the kitten was the right thing to do. It didn't have identification. Megan, go over to Tim's and get the kitten back. Then I'll call the number on the sign."

Megan whined, "I don't want to!"

Her mother said, "Think how you'd feel if Fluffo got lost. And someone found him and gave him away. And didn't call you. Even if your number was on a sign right outside their house."

Megan exclaimed, "I'd be really mad!"

"Go get the kitten," said her mother.

Megan did not want to do that. She pouted. Then she went to find Fluffo. He was snoozing on his favorite chair by a sunny window.

She picked him up and held him on her lap. He nuzzled her arm. She scratched under his chin. He purred loudly. He sounded as if he had a little motor in his throat.

Megan thought about losing Fluffo. She thought about someone giving him away to a new home. She sighed.

"Megan!" called her mother.

"Okay," she answered. "I'm going."

Annie and Susie went along.

"Tim's going to be really mad," warned Annie.

On the way, they passed Eric's yard. The boys' snowman was much bigger than the snermaid. He wore a baseball cap. A hockey stick leaned against him.

"That's a really good snowman," said Susie.

"No hair," remarked Annie. "I thought they'd copy us."

At Tim's they saw a snow wall about four feet high in the front yard. The boys were nowhere to be seen.

"They must be in the house," said Megan, "with the kitten."

When they got close to the wall, Susie said, "I hear whispering!"

"Duck!" yelled Megan. Snowballs flew from behind the wall. Some missed. Some splattered on the girls' coats.

"Let's get 'em!" yelled Susie. The girls scooped up handfuls of snow. They charged the fort. They threw lots of snow over the wall.

"You missed!" hollered Eric. The girls ran around the wall. They all threw more snow at each other. They rolled around, ducking and laughing.

Soon they all looked like snowboys and snowgirls. Their hats, coats, mittens, and boots were crusted with snow. Their cheeks were rosy.

Their noses were getting numb. But they didn't feel cold.

"Truce!" exclaimed Tim. "But we got you good!"

"We got you good, too," said Susie.

Annie looked around the boys' fort. "Room dividers!" she said. "You copied us!"

Susie reminded Megan, "Tell them about the sign."

Megan explained.

Tim looked very upset. "I'm not giving Batster Catster back!" he said.

"But you have to," said Megan.

"No, I don't," replied Tim, frowning. "You gave him to me. He's mine."

"But —" said Megan.

"No way!" said Tim. He stomped off into his house.

"No fair!" agreed Eric. He stomped off after Tim.

"Rats!" said Megan.

"They're really mad," said Annie.

The girls walked home slowly. When they were almost there, they heard a shout far behind them. "Wait up!" called Tim. He and Eric hurried to catch up.

Tim's coat was not zipped up all the way. A little furry gray face peeked out.

"My mom says I have to give him back," he told Megan. "She said it's not your fault."

At Megan's, her mother called the number on the sign.

"We found a gray kitten last night," she said on the phone. "Yes, it sounds like the one you lost. Oh, really? No, we don't want to keep him. But we know someone who does."

When she hung up, she told Tim, "He's yours to keep."

Megan asked, "Why didn't they want him back?"

Her mother replied, "Because their cat had a litter of five kittens. They need to find homes for all five. They put up some signs because they wanted to make sure the lost one was found."

Eric said, "Maybe I could get one."

Megan's mother gave Eric the phone number.

Mike was counting the money he earned snowblowing. He asked the girls, "Did you see the weird tracks in the backyard?"

"What kind are they?" asked Susie.

"I don't know," he replied. "They're the strangest ones I've ever seen."

"Maybe it's the green hair stealer monster," said Susie, laughing.

"The what?" asked Mike. The girls did not explain. They just giggled.

"If I didn't know better," said Mike, "I'd think it could be a polar bear."

"It couldn't be," said Annie.

"Well, go and look for yourself," said Mike. "They're pretty big tracks."

The girls headed for the back door.

"Be careful," Mike called after them, "in case it's a polar bear!"

Megan said, "Don't pay any attention to him. He's just trying to scare us." She yelled back at Mike, "We're not scared!"

The strange tracks started halfway across the yard. They were different from the many boot tracks where Megan's family had walked through the yard. These were oval and about twelve inches wide.

"It took big steps," said Susie. "The tracks are far apart. Not the way we walk."

Annie said, "It's definitely not a polar bear."

"No, these don't look like paw prints," said Megan. "They're smooth. Like metal."

Annie said, "Like robot feet!"

Megan looked back at the kitchen window. Mike and Fluffo were watching them. Mike was grinning.

"I think he's trying to trick us," said Megan. "But I don't know how."

"Do you think he built a robot?" asked Susie.

"Maybe," said Megan. "Maybe not."

Susie's parents invited a lot of the neighbors over for a potluck supper. Every family brought something different to eat. The kitchen smelled delicious.

When Eric arrived, his coat was not zipped up all the way. A little furry orange face peeked out.

"You got a kitten!" exclaimed Megan. Everyone gathered around to "ooh" and "aah."

"What's his name?" asked Annie.

"Soopie," replied Eric. "That's his nickname. His real name is Supercat."

Tim had brought Batster Catster, too. Pud sniffed the kittens. But they were not afraid of him. Susie gave him a pat. He curled up in a corner to get out of the way of all the feet.

The children were running through the house, laughing and shouting.

"Settle down," Susie's dad told them.

After they ate, the grown-ups sat around talking about the big snow.

"This is nothing," said Annie's father. "I grew up in North Dakota. Now *that's* big snow. Sometimes we were snowed in for days. It was so cold one time that my nose froze and fell off. I didn't find it until all the snow melted in the spring."

"That's not really true," said Tim, chuckling.

"It's a tall tale," said Annie. "He likes to tell tall tales."

Her father patted his nose. "It looks as good as new, though, doesn't it?" Everyone laughed.

Megan said, "I know a tall tale. There was a robot in our backyard today. It left big smooth footprints!"

"That's a good one," said Annie's father.

Mrs. Johnson said, "I saw your robot."

"You did?" asked Megan. She looked very surprised.

Mrs. Johnson smiled at Mike. "He looked exactly like your brother," she told Megan. "I wondered why he was taking such big steps around the yard. Then I saw that he had his feet in wastebaskets."

Mike laughed. "I fooled everybody," he said.

"No, you didn't," insisted Megan. "We knew you were tricking us."

"Yeah," said Annie.

Tim said, "That's a good trick. I wish I'd thought of that."

"Me, too," said Eric.

As everyone was leaving to walk home, it was starting to snow again.

Megan said, "Maybe we'll have another snow day tomorrow."

"I hope so," said Susie.

Other *Adventure* books by Nancy McArthur

The Adventure of the Buried Treasure
The Adventure of the Backyard Sleepout